Copyright © 2005 by Lemniscaat b.v. Rotterdam
Originally published in the Netherlands by Lemniscaat b.v. Rotterdam
under the title *Broertje*
All rights reserved
Printed in Belgium
CIP data available
First U.S. edition

Baby Brother

Tanneke Wigersma & Nynke Mare Talsma

Front Street 8 Lemniscaat

Dear Grandma, how are you?

I am fine.

Stripe walked around with a big belly for weeks,

but she wasn't eating her own food.

She couldn't jump anymore, so I had to help.

And she used to be scared of the neighbor's dog.

But then it was the other way around.

Yesterday, Stripe was meowing a lot.

She tried to get

into

and

under

everything.

I made her a special box.

In the evening, she got into her box.

Within an hour she had five little Stripes. Very cute!

By the way, I also have a new baby brother.

Love and kisses, Mia.